by Alvin Tresselt
illustrated by Roger Duvoisin

What Did You Leave Behind?

Lothrop, Lee & Shepard Company, A Division of William Morrow & Company, Inc., New York

For Christopher Lep
In Remembrance

The seashore sand has come home in your sneakers, between your toes, in your hair, and damp and sticky on a beach towel.

The empty seashell homes of snails,
the lost brown shell of a crab,
and a crusty dried starfish, you carried in a pail.
But what did you leave at the beach?

Did you leave the hot scent of wild roses...
the cool tingle of the salt spray?
Did you leave the sunlight dancing on blue water?

Did you leave the thunder-crash of great waves,
stumbling and spilling on the smooth wet sand?
The dry rusty whisper of beach grasses…

the complaining skreek of seagulls...
and the taste of salt...
Did you *really* leave all these behind?

The parade swings down the street
with a blare of trumpets,
the golden clash of cymbals,

the deep bass rumble of the tuba
and the boom of the big round drum.

Flags waving, men and women marching,
and horses gaily prancing.

Then home you go with a sassy balloon on a string,
and a proud flag all red, white and blue.
But what did the parade take away
as it went on down the street?

Did it take away the sound of marching feet?
Did it take away the band?
The shrill cry of the piccolo...
The rat-a-tat-tat of the drummers...
and the golden clash of the cymbals...

Do you still feel the beat and tingle in your toes?
Does the music echo in your ears?
Are the flags still waving when you close your eyes?
Did the parade *really* take all this away?

In your hand you hold a bunch of violets for your mother,
a piece of soft green moss for her to feel,
a long black crow's feather for your collection of things,

and a pretty pebble for your sister to put in her collection.
But did you leave something behind,
back there in the woods, far across the fields?

Did you leave the spring song of birds?
The conversation of frogs…
the water singing in the brook…
the musty-moisty smell of wet dead leaves
and rotting wood…

Did you bring back the sunlight coming down all speckled
through the new green of young leaves…
the sharp hoofprints there in the mud
beside the brook where a mother deer stopped to drink
with her baby…
Did you *really* leave these back in the woods
on a soft spring day?

In you come, with snow inside your boots,
soggy wet mittens and a cherry-red nose.
Unwrap, unzip, undo, and there you are,

ready for hot chocolate and cookies.
But did you leave something out there
in the white winter world?

Did you leave the angels you made
when you flip-flapped your arms and legs
in a snowbank?

What about the ice creaking on the tree branches
as the wind went by…
The sun-sparkle on the ice,
setting the trees ablaze with Christmas lights…

the cold sting of a snowball...
the zip of a sled flying down the hill...
Did you really leave all these outside?

Home at last from the fair, and you're ready for bed.
There's a bird on a string at the end of a stick,
resting in the corner,
and a big stuffed lion sitting on the bed
waiting for you to hop in.
(Your father won it for you in the dart game.)
And your fingers still feel sticky
from the cotton candy.
But what did you leave at the fair?

Did you leave the smell of hot dogs and pizza...
the bubbly tickle of ice-cold soda...
the up-and-down and umpa-ump of the merry-go-round...

the dizzy swing at the top of the ferris wheel...

Did you leave the pungent smell of cows and horses
in the barns...

the raucous crow of proud roosters…
the wooly feel of a sheep's back…

the contented grunts
of the mother pig with all her piglets...
Did you *really* leave all these behind at the fair?